William McLennan

Songs of old Canada

William McLennan

Songs of old Canada

ISBN/EAN: 9783744769846

Printed in Europe, USA, Canada, Australia, Japan

Cover: Foto ©Andreas Hilbeck / pixelio.de

More available books at **www.hansebooks.com**

SONGS OF

.

OLD CANADA.

TRANSLATED BY

WILLIAM McLENNAN.

"*Le Canadien mêlait* . . . . . .
Ses chants d'amour et ses refrains joyeux."

M. A. PLAMONDON.

MONTREAL :
DAWSON BROTHERS, PUBLISHERS.
1886.

PREFACE.

Many of these translations were published during the course of the present year in the column of *Ephemerides* in the Montreal *Gazette*, and were written in response to an enquiry for English translations of the old Canadian songs.

The object of the translator has been to present, in an English dress and in a form that will allow of their being sung to the airs which most of us have heard with delight, a few of the more popular and striking of those songs of Old France, so wonderfully preserved by our song-loving countrymen. Of these, many have disappeared in their mother-country, and in nearly all of them changes and corruptions have debased either the words or the air. It is also to be feared, alas! that even in the Province of Quebec, which has been their ark of safety for so long, some of them are being forgotten.

The selections that have been made are those which appeared to the translator to offer the best opportunity for successful treatment in another language; while some of the most popular songs, such as *A Saint-Malo, Marianne s'en va-t-au Moulin* and *La belle Françoise*, have been most unwillingly passed over, on account either of the form or the subject. When one remembers the difficulty of sustained rhyming in our language, and the absolute necessity of it in such songs as these, the repetition of terminal words and phrases which occurs will be understood.

It will be noticed that most of the songs bear only their first line by way of title, but in this M. Gagnon has been followed, and it must be remembered that he took down the songs as he heard them sung by the people. Few of them had ever been printed, and fewer still had names.

Those who are interested in the subject, will find a rich store of information in *Les Chansons populaires du Canada* by M. Ernest Gagnon, an invaluable work the second edition of which was published by Robert Morgan, Quebec, in 1880, and, in an able and useful article by Dr. Larue, in the *Foyer Canadien* of 1863. To these sources the translator is deeply indebted both for the original text and for much of the information contained in the notes.

Montreal, December 1st, 1885.

CONTENTS.

I've tried to waken with a loving care
Some echo of the joyance of these lays,
Which sound as sweetly on Canadian air,
As 'neath the skies of France in olden days.

How often has each song been lightly sung
By lips that now are silent for all time !
How often has each tender cadence flung
O'er distant seas the magic of its chime !

Oblivion's self was softened by their grace
And stored them safe within a people's heart,
To share the fortunes of a songful race,
And charm us with the artlessness of Art.

A LA CLAIRE FONTAINE.

A la claire fontaine
    M'en allant promener,
J'ai trouvé l'eau si belle
    Que je m'y suis baigné.
        I' y a longtemps que je t'aime,
        Jamais je ne t'oublierai.

J'ai trouvé l'eau si belle
    Que je m'y suis baigné,
Et c'est au pied d'un chêne
    Que je m'suis reposé.

Et c'est au pied d'un chêne
    Que je m'suis reposé :
Sur la plus haute branche
    Le rossignol chantait.

A LA CLAIRE FONTAINE.

Down to the crystal streamlet
　　I strayed at close of day ;
Into its limpid waters,
　　I plunged without delay.
　　　　I've loved thee long and dearly,
　　　　I'll love thee, Sweet, for aye.

Into its limpid waters,
　　I plunged without delay ;
Then mid the flowers springing
　　At the oak-tree's foot I lay.

Then mid the flowers springing
　　At the oak-tree's foot I lay ;
Sweet the nightingale was singing,
　　High on the topmost spray.

3

Sur la plus haute branche
  Le rossignol chantait ;
Chante rossignol, chante,
  Toi qui as le cœur gai.

Chante rossignol, chante,
  Toi qui as le cœur gai ;
Tu as le cœur à rire,
  Moi je l'ai-t-à pleurer.

Tu as le cœur à rire,
  Moi je l'ai-t-à pleurer ;
J'ai perdu ma maîtresse
  Sans pouvoir la trouver.

J'ai perdu ma maîtresse
  Sans pouvoir la trouver ;
Pour un bouquet de roses
  Que je lui refusai.

Pour un bouquet de roses
  Que je lui refusai ;
Je voudrais que la rose
  Fût encore au rosier.

Sweet the nightingale was singing,
  High on the topmost spray ;
Sweet bird ! keep ever ringing
  Thy song with heart so gay.

Sweet bird ! keep ever ringing
  Thy song with heart so gay ;
Thy heart was made for laughter,
  My heart's in tears to-day.

Thy heart was made for laughter,
  My heart's in tears to-day ;
Tears for a fickle mistress,
  Flown from its love away.

In tears for a fickle mistress,
  Flown from its love away,
All for these faded roses
  Which I refused in play.

All for these faded roses
  Which I refused in play—
Would that each rose were growing
  Still on the rose tree gay !

Je voudrais que la rose
  Fût encore au rosier,
Et que le rosier même
  Fût dans la mer jeté.

> *I' ya longtemps que je t'aime,*
> *`Jamais je ne t'oublierai.*

A LA CLAIRE FONTAINE.

Would that each rose were growing
 Still on the rose tree gay,
And that the fatal rose tree
 Deep in the ocean lay !

> *I've loved thee long and dearly,*
> *I'll love thee, Sweet, for aye.*

MALBROUCK.

MALBROUCK s'en va-t-en guerre,
    Mironton, mironton, mirontaine,
Malbrouck s'en va-t-en guerre,
Ne sait quand reviendra.

Il reviendra-z-à Pâques,
Ou à la Trinité.

La Trinité se passe,
Malbrouck ne revient pas.

Madame à sa tour monte,
Si haut qu'ell' peut monter.

Elle aperçoit son page
Tout de noir habillé.

MALBROUCK.

MALBROUCK has gone a-fighting,
 Mironton, mironton, mirontaine;
Malbrouck has gone a-fighting
But when will he return ?

Perchance he'll come at Easter
Or else at Trinity Term.

But Trinity Term is over
And Malbrouck comes not yet.

My Lady climbs her watch tower
As high as she can get.

She sees her page approaching
All clad in sable hue :

9

Beau page, ah ! mon beau page,
Quell' nouvelle apportez ?

Aux nouvell's que j'apporte,
Vos beaux yeux vont pleurer.

Quittez vos habits roses,
Et vos satins brochés.

Monsieur Malbrouck est mort,
Est mort et enterré.

Je l'ai vu porter en terre,
Par quatre-z-officiers.

L'un portait sa cuirasse,
L'autre son bouclier.

L'un portait son grand sabre,
L'autre ne portait rien.

A l'entour de sa tombe,
Romarins l'on planta.

' Ah page, brave page, what tidings
From my true lord bring you ? "

" The news I bring, fair Lady,
Will make your tears run down ;

" Put off your rose-red dress so fine
And doff your satin gown.

" Monsieur Malbrouck is dead, alas !
And buried too, for aye ;

" I saw four officers who bore
His mighty corse away.

" One bore his cuirass, and his friend
His shield of iron wrought ;

" The third his mighty sabre bore,
And the fourth—he carried nought.

" And at the corners of his tomb
They planted rose-marie ;

Sur la plus haute branche,
Le rossignol chanta.

On vit voler son âme,
A travers des lauriers.

Chacun mit ventre à terre,
Et puis se releva.

Pour chanter les victoires,
Que Malbrouck remporta.

La cérémoni' faite,
Chacun s'en fut s'coucher.

J'n'en dis pas davantage
          Mironton, mironton, mirontaine,
J'n'en dis pas davantage
Car en voilà z-assez.

" And from their tops the nightingale
Rings out her carol free.

" We saw, above the laurels,
His soul fly forth amain ;

" And each one fell upon his face
And then rose up again.

" And so we sang the glories
For which great Malbrouck bled ;

" And when the whole was ended
Each one went off to bed.

" I say no more, my Lady,
     Mironton, mironton, mirontaine,
I say no more, my Lady,
As nought more can be said."

LE POMMIER DOUX.

Par derrier' chez mon père,
  Vole, mon cœur, vole,
Par derrier' chez mon père,
I' ya-t-un pommier doux ;
  Tout doux,
I' ya-t-un pommier doux.

Les feuilles en sont vertes,
  Vole, mon cœur, vole,
Les feuilles en sont vertes
Et le fruit en est doux ;
  Tout doux,
Et le fruit en est doux.

14

LE POMMIER DOUX.

A<small>N</small> apple tree there groweth,
        Fly away, my heart, away;
An apple tree there groweth
Within my father's close ;
        So sweet,
Within my father's close.

Oh, bright is every leaf thereon,
        Fly away, my heart, away ;
Oh, bright is every leaf thereon
And sweet the fruit that grows
        So sweet,
And sweet the fruit that grows.

15

Nos amants sont en guerre,
　　　　　Vole, mon cœur, vole,
Nos amants sont en guerre
Ils combattent pour nous ;
　　　　　Tout doux,
Ils combattent pour nous.

Trois filles d'un prince,
　　　　　Vole, mon cœur, vole,
Trois filles d'un prince
Sont endormies dessous ;
　　　　　Tout doux,
Sont endormies dessous.

La plus jeun' se réveille,
　　　　　Vole, mon cœur, vole,
La plus jeun' se réveille :
— Ma sœur, voilà le jour ;
　　　　　Tout doux,
Ma sœur, voilà le jour.

The King's three lovely daughters,
  Fly away, my heart, away ;
The King's three lovely daughters
Beneath its branches lay,
  So sweet,
Beneath its branches lay.

The youngest wakens lightly,
  Fly away, my heart, away ;
The youngest wakens lightly :
" My sister, here is day !
  So sweet,
" My sister, here is day ! "

" T'is but a star that's gilding,
  Fly away, my heart, away ;
" T'is but a star that's gilding
With its sweet light our love,
  So sweet,
" With its sweet light our love."

— Non, ce n'est qu'une étoile,

        Vole, mon cœur, vole,

Non, ce n'est qu'une étoile

Qu'éclaire nos amours ;

        Tout doux,

Qu'éclaire nos amours.

S'ils gagnent la bataille,

        Vole, mon cœur, vole,

S'ils gagnent la bataille,

Ils auront nos amours ;

        Tout doux,

Ils auront nos amours.

Qu'ils perdent ou qu'ils gagnent,

        Vole, mon cœur, vole,

Qu'ils perdent ou qu'ils gagnent,

Ils les auront toujours ;

        Tout doux,

Ils les auront toujours.

" Our lovers ride to battle,
  Fly away, my heart, away;
Our lovers ride to battle
Their love for us to prove,
  So sweet,
Their love for us to prove."

" And if they gain the battle,
  Fly away, my heart, away;
And if they gain the battle,
Our love shall crown the day,
  So sweet,
Our love shall crown the day."

" Oh, let them win or let them fail,
  Fly away, my heart, away;
Oh, let them win or let them fail,
Our love is theirs alway,
  So sweet,
Our love is theirs alway."

EN ROULANT MA BOULE.

D ERRIÈR' chez nous, ya-t-un étang,
  En roulant ma boule.
Trois beaux canards s'en vont baignant,
  En roulant ma boule.
    Rouli, roulant, ma boule roulant,
    En roulant ma boule roulant,
    En roulant ma boule.

Trois beaux canards s'en vont baignant,
Le fils du roi s'en va chassant.

Le fils du roi s'en va chassant
Avec son grand fusil d'argent.

Avec son grand fusil d'argent
Visa le noir, tua le blanc.

EN ROULANT MA BOULE.

BEHIND the Manor lies the mere,
 En roulant ma boule;
Three ducks bathe in its water clear,
 En roulant ma boule.
  Rouli, roulant, ma boule roulant,
  En roulant ma boule roulant,
  En roulant ma boule.

Three fairy ducks swim without fear :
The Prince goes hunting far and near.

The Prince at last draws near the lake :
He bears his gun of magic make.

With magic gun of silver bright,
He sights the Black but kills the White.

21

Visa le noir, tua le blanc :
O fils du roi, tu es méchant !

—O fils du roi, tu es méchant
D'avoir tué mon canard blanc !

D'avoir tué mon canard blanc,
Par dessous l'aile il perd son sang,

Par dessous l'aile il perd son sang,
Par les yeux lui sort'nt des diamants.

Par les yeux lui sort'nt des diamants,
Et par le bec l'or et l'argent.

Et par le bec l'or et l'argent,
Toutes ses plum's s'en vont au vent.

Toutes ses plum's s'en vont au vent,
Trois dam's s'en vont les ramassant

Trois dam's s'en vont les ramassant,
C'est pour en faire un lit de camp.

He sights the Black but kills the White :
Ah ! cruel Prince, my heart you smite.

Ah ! cruel Prince, my heart you break,
In killing thus my snow-white Drake.

My snow-white Drake, my Love, my King ;
The crimson life-blood stains his wing.

His life-blood falls in rubies bright,
His diamond eyes have lost their light.

The cruel ball has found its quest,
His golden bill sinks on his breast.

His golden bill sinks on his breast,
His plumes go floating East and West.

Far, far they're borne to distant lands,
Till gathered by fair maidens' hands ;

Till gathered by fair maidens' hands ;
And form at last a soldier's bed.

C'est pour en faire un lit de camp,
En roulant ma boule.
Pour y coucher tous les passants
En roulant ma boule.

Rouli, roulant, ma boule roulant,
En roulant ma boule roulant,
En roulant ma boule.

And form at last a soldier's bed,
   En roulant ma boule;
Sweet refuge for the wanderer's head,
   En roulant ma boule.

   Rouli, roulant, ma boule roulant,
   En roulant ma boule roulant,
   En roulant ma boule.

GAI LE ROSIER.

Par derrièr' chez ma tante
  I' ya-t-un bois joli ;
Le rossignol y chante
Et le jour et la nuit.
  Gai lon la, gai le rosier
  Du joli mois de mai.

Le rossignol y chante
Et le jour et la nuit.
Il chante pour ces belles
Qui n'ont pas de mari.

Il chante pour ces belles
Qui n'ont pas de mari,
Il ne chant' pas pour moi
Car j'en ai-t-un joli.

GAI LE ROSIER.

BEHIND my aunt's there groweth
    A wood all greenery ;
The nightingale's song filleth
    Its glades with melodie.
        Gai lon la, gai le rosier
        Du joli mois de mai.

The nightingale's song filleth
    Its glades with melodie ;
He sings for maids whose beauty
    No lover holds in fee.

He sings for maids whose beauty
    No lover holds in fee ;
For me he singeth never,
    For my True-love loves me.

27

Il ne chant' pas pour moi
Car j'en ai-t-un joli :
Il n'est point dans la danse,
Il est bien loin d'ici.

Il n'est point dans la danse
Il est bien loin d'ici ;
Il est dans la Hollande :
Les Hollandais l'ont pris.

Il est dans la Hollande :
Les Hollandais l'ont pris.
— Que donneriez-vous, belle,
Qui l'amen'rait ici ?

Que donneriez-vous, belle,
Qui l'amen'rait ici ?
— Je donnerais Versailles,
Paris et Saint-Denis.

Je donnerais Versailles,
Paris et Saint-Denis
Et la claire fontaine
Dans mon jardin joli.

Gai lon la, gai le rosier
Du joli mois de mai.

For me he singeth never
  For my True-love loves me ;
He joins no more the dancers,
  Alas ! he's far from me.

He joins no more the dancers,
  Alas ! he's far from me,
A prisoner ta'en while fighting
  In distant Germanie.

A prisoner ta'en while fighting
  In distant Germanie.
" What wilt thou give, sweet maiden,
  An I bring him back to thee ? "

" What wilt thou give, sweet maiden,
  An I bring him back to thee ? "
" I'll give thee all Versailles,
  Paris and St. Denis."

" I'll give thee all Versailles,
  Paris and St. Denis,
And the crystal fount that floweth
  In my garden clear and free."

    Gai lon la, gai le rosier
    Du joli mois de mai.

BRIGADIER.

Deux gendarmes, un beau dimanche ;
  Chevauchaient le long du sentier ;
L'un portait la sardine blanche,
L'autre le jaune baudrier.
Le premier dit d'un ton sonore,
Le temps est beau pour la saison.
      Brigadier, répondit Pandore,
      Brigadier vous avez raison.

Ah ! c'est un métier difficile,
Garantir la propriété,
Protéger les champs et la ville
Du vol et de l'iniquité.
Pourtant l'épouse que j'adore
Repose seule à la maison.
      Brigadier, répondit Pandore,
      Brigadier vous avez raison.

BRIGADIER.

T wo men-at-arms came riding slowly
    Adown the green path, smooth and clear ;
One held the rank of sergeant lowly,
    The other that of brigadier.
The brigadier cried, " Brave Pandore,
    The weather's fine—no signs of rain."
        " Brigadier," laughing cried Pandore,
        " Brigadier, right you are again !"

" It is no easy matter, surely,
    To guard the peasant in his cot,
To hold the cities so securely
    That thieves break in and plunder not ;
And yet the wife whom I adore,
    In safety dwells where Love doth reign."
        " Brigadier," laughing cried Pandore,
        " Brigadier, right you are again !"

La gloire, c'est une couronne
Faite de rose et de laurier ;
J'ai servi Vénus et Bellone,
Je suis époux et brigadier ;
Mais je poursuis ce météore
Qui vers Chalcos, guida Jason.

     Brigadier, répondit Pandore,
     Brigadier vous avez raison.

Je me souviens de ma jeunesse,
Le temps passé ne revient pas,
J'avais une folle maîtresse
Pleine de mérites et d'appas.
Mais le cœur, pourquoi, je l'ignore
Aime à changer la garnison.

     Brigadier, répondit Pandore,
     Brigadier vous avez raison.

Phébus au bout de sa carrière
Put encor les apercevoir ;
Le brigadier de sa voix fière,
Réveillait les échos du soir :

" For Glory's wreath of fairest flowers
 With rose and laurel intertwined ;
For Love and War, immortal powers,
 I live—and cast the rest behind.
The Power that Jason led of yore
 I chase and trust the prize to gain."

    " Brigadier," laughing cried Pandore,
    " Brigadier, right you are again ! "

" It brings bright days of youth before me ;
 That Past now gone beyond recall,
When Beauty flung her fetters o'er me,
 I came submissive to her call.
And yet—the heart breaks o'er and o'er
 The strongest links of Cupid's chain."

    " Brigadier," laughing cried Pandore,
    " Brigadier, right you are again."

As Phœbus hid his glories under
 The golden clouds that veil the West,
Our hero with his voice of thunder
 Still broke the evening's quiet rest.

C

Je vois, dit-il, le soleil qui dore
Ces verts côteaux à l'horizon.

> *Brigadier, répondit Pandore,*
> *Brigadier vous avez raison.*

Puis ils cheminèrent en silence ;
On n'entendit plus que le pas
Des chevaux marchant en cadence,
Le brigadier ne parlait pas ;
Mais quand parût la pâle aurore,
On entendit un vague son ;

> *Brigadier, répondit Pandore,*
> *Brigadier vous avez raison.*

" Farewell ! " he cried, " on distant shore
  Your light will gild both hill and plain."

    " Brigadier," laughing cried Pandore,
    " Brigadier, right you are again ! "

He ceased—and now their horses tramping
  Fell softly on the yielding ground,
And save their iron bridles champing,
  They passed along and made no sound ;
But when Aurora smiled once more
  One still might hear the faint refrain—

    " Brigadier," laughing cried Pandore,
    " Brigadier, right you are again ! "

Dans les prisons de Nantes
    I' ya-t-un prisonnier,
        Gai, faluron, falurette.
I' ya-t-un prisonnier.
        Gai, faluron, dondé.

Que personn' ne va voir
Que la fill' du geôlier.

Elle lui porte à boire
A boire et à manger.

Un jour il lui demande :
— Qu'est-c' que l'on dit de moi ?

Le bruit court dans la ville
Que demain vous mourrez.

36

DANS LES PRISONS DE NANTES.

I N prison cell at Nantes
   A hapless prisoner lay,
        Gai, faluron, falurette,
A hapless prisoner lay.
        Gai, faluron, dondé.

No human soul came nigh him,
Save the jailor's daughter gay :

With her fair hands supplying
His prison fare each day.

One morn he cried, half sighing:
" What do the gossips say ? "

" Alas, they say to-morrow
Will be your dying day."

37

— Puisqu'il faut que je meure,
Ah ! déliez-moi les pieds.

La fille encore jeunette,
Lui a lâché les pieds.

Le garçon fort alerte,
A la mer s'est jeté.

De la première plonge
Au fond il a été.

De la seconde plonge
La mer a traversé.

Quand il fut sur ces côtes,
Il se mit à chanter :

— Que Dieu béniss' les filles
Surtout cell' du geôlier.

Si je retourne à Nantes,
Oui, je l'épouserai,
    Gai, faluron, falurette,
Oui, je l'épouserai,
    Gai, faluron, dondè.

" Since death is now so near me
Undo these bonds, I pray."

She, strong in youth's sweet pity,
Broke all his bonds away.

He, brave in youth's bold daring,
Leaped far into the bay.

His first wild plunge has borne him
Deep 'neath the waters grey.

The second bears him safe across
The wild sea's dashing spray.

In safety now he boldly stands
And carols forth this lay :—

" God bless all maidens fair, but most,
The jailor's daughter gay ;

And should I e'er return to Nantes
I'll wed her, yea or nay,
  Gai, faluron, falurette,
I'll wed her, yea or nay."
  Gai, faluron, dondé.

CÉCILIA.

M^{on} pèr' n'avait fille que moi
   Encor sur la mer il m'envoie.
Sautez, mignonne Cécilia,
Ah ! ah, Cécilia.

Encor sur la mer il m'envoie.
Le marinier qui m'y menait—

Le marinier qui m'y menait,
Il devint amoureux de moi.

Il devint amoureux de moi.
— Ma mignonnette, embrassez-moi.

Ma mignonnette, embrassez-moi.
— Nenni, Monsieur, je n'oserais.

Nenni, Monsieur, je n'oserais,
Car si mon papa le savait.

CECILIA.

ALTHOUGH my father's only child,
He sent me o'er the ocean wild.
Sautez mignonne Cecilia,
Ah! ah, Cecilia!

Over the seas and far away
Borne by a sailor bold and gay.

Borne by a sailor bold and gay,
Who fell in love with me each day.

He fell in love with me each day :
"Ah, Sweet! one little kiss I pray."

"One little kiss for all my care."
"Alas! alas! I'd never dare."

"For if I did," she whispered low,
"My cruel father 'd surely know."

41

Car si mon papa le savait,
Fille battue ce serait moi.

Fille battue ce serait moi.
— Voulez-vous bell' qui lui dirait ?

Voulez-vous bell' qui lui dirait ?
— Ce serait les oiseaux des bois.

Ce serait les oiseaux des bois.
— Les oiseaux dés bois parlent-ils ?

Les oiseaux des bois parlent-ils ?
— Ils parl'nt français, latin aussi.

Ils parl'nt français, latin aussi.
— Hélas ! que le monde est malin :

Hélas ! que le monde est malin
D'apprendre aux oiseaux le latin !

Sautez, mignonne Cécilia,
Ah ! ah, Cécilia.

" And should he know your love for me,
A sorely punished maid I'd be."

" Now, foolish maid, we're far away,
How could your father know, I pray?"

" How could my father know, you say?
He'd hear it from the wood doves grey."

" But even though the doves might sing,
He'd never know the tale they bring."

" He would not understand, think you?
They speak good French—and Latin too."

" Now may his evil neck be wrung
Who taught the doves the Latin tongue!"
    Sautez mignonne Cecilia,
    Ah! ah, Cecilia!

C'ETAIT UNE FREGATE.

C'ÉTAIT une frégate,
  Mon joli cœur de rose,
Dans la mer a touché,
  Joli cœur d'un rosier.

Y'avait un' demoiselle
Su' l'bord d'la mer pleurait.

— Dites-moi donc, la belle,
Qu'a-vous à tant pleurer ?

— Je pleur' mon anneau d'or,
Dans la mer est tombé.

— Que donneriez-vous, belle,
Qu' irait vous le chercher ?

— Je suis trop pauvre fille,
Je ne puis rien donner

44

C'ETAIT UNE FREGATE.

A frigate went a-sailing,
   Mon joli cœur de rose,
Far o'er the seas away,
   Joli cœur d'un rosier.

A gentle maid was weeping
Beside the smiling bay.

" Ah, tell me, Sweet, what sorrow
Bedims your eyes to-day? "

" Ah, Sir, I've lost my ring of gold
Deep 'neath the waters grey."

" And if I find it, gentle maid,
What will you give, I pray? "

" Alas, kind Sir, I'm poor, and nought
Have I to give away ;

Qu' mon cœur en mariage
Pour mon anneau doré.

Le galant se dépouille,
Dans la mer s'est jeté.

De la première plonge
L'anneau d'or a touché.

De la seconde plonge
L'anneau d'or a sonné.

De la troisième plonge,
Le galant s'est noyé.

Il allait à la d'rive
Comme un poisson doré.

Son pèr' sur la fenêtre,
Le regardait d'river.

— Faut-il, pour une fille,
　　Mon joli cœur de rose.
Que mon fils soit noyé.
　　Joli cœur d'un rosier.

"Unless my heart is wage enough
For my ring beneath the bay."

He threw his cloak aside and plunged
Deep where the jewel lay.

The first strong plunge he almost touched
The golden ring so gay.

The second time, it moved and rang,
But lured him on alway.

But at the third, the lover bold
Was drowned. Ah, mournful day!

And with the tide that gallant heart
Swept seaward o'er the bay.

His father from his turret sees
And bows his head so grey.

"Alas, that for a maid, my son,
      Mon joli cœur de rose,
Should throw his life away,
      Joli cœur d'un rosier!"

E NTRE Paris et Saint-Denis
    Il s'élève une danse ;
Toutes les dames de la ville
Sont alentour qui dansent.
      Sur la feuille ron… don don don,
      Sur la joli', joli' feuille ronde.

Toutes les dames de la ville
Sont alentour qui dansent,
Il n'y a que la fill' du roi
D'un côté qui regarde.

Il n'y a que la fill' du roi
D'un côté qui regarde.
Ell' voit venir son messager,
Son messager de Nantes.

, TWIXT Paris fair and St. Denis
The dance was up one day,
And all the ladies of the town
Looked on in brave array.

> *Sur la feuille ron... don don don,*
> *Sur la joli', joli' feuille ronde.*

And all the ladies of the town
Looked on in brave array,
All save the Princess fair, who glanced
Adown the dusty way.

The Princess fair cast wistful looks
Adown the dusty way,
And soon she saw her messenger
Ride from where Nantés lay.

D   49

Ell' voit venir son messager,
Son messager de Nantes.
— Beau messager, beau messager,
Quell's nouvell's ya à Nantes ?

Beau messager, beau messager,
Quell's nouvell's ya à Nantes ?
— Les nouvell's que j'ai apportées :
Que votre amant vous mande—

Les͏ nouvell's que j'ai apportées :
Que votre amant vous mande
Que vous fassiez choix d'un amant,
Pour lui a une amante.

Que vous fassiez choix d'un amant,
Pour lui a une amante.
— Est-elle plus belle que moi ?
Est-elle plus savante ?

Est-elle plus belle que moi ?
Est-elle plus savante ?
— Ell' n'est pas plus belle que toi,
Mais elle est plus savante.

She saw her faithful messenger
His way from Nantés wing :
" Now, Messenger, from Nantés town,
What tidings do you bring ? "

" Now Messenger, bold Messenger,
What news from Nantés fair ?"
" The only news I bring, fair Dame,
Your lover bade me bear.

" The only news I bring is this —
Your lover bade me say,
'That he has found a sweetheart new,
Choose you a gallant gay.

" Choose you another gallant gay
For I've a sweetheart rare."
— " Now is she wiser far than I,
Or is her face more fair ?"

" Now is she wiser far than I
Or is her face more fair ?"
" Although, not near so fair as you,
Her wisdom's past compare.

Ell' n'est pas plus belle que toi,
Mais elle est plus savante :
Ell' fait neiger, ell' fait grêler,
Ell' fait le vent qui vente.

Ell' fait neiger, ell' fait grêler,
Ell' fait le vent qui vente ;
Ell' fait reluire le soleil
A minuit dans sa chambre.

Ell' fait reluire le soleil
A minuit dans sa chambre ;
Ell' fait pousser le romarin
Sur le bord de la Manche.

> *Sur la feuille ron... don don don,*
> *Sur la joli', joli' feuille ronde.*

"' Her beauty is not like to yours
But secret lore she knows,
She makes the snow, she makes the hail,
She makes the wind that blows.

" She makes the wind that blows so free,
She makes the snow so fine,
At midnight hour, within her bower,
She makes the sun to shine.

"' She makes the sun to shine again
At midnight in her bower,
And on the borders of the sea
Makes rosemary to flower."

> *Sur la feuille ron... don don don,*
> *Sur la joli', joli' feuille ronde.*

MARIANSON.

— Marianson, dame jolie,
Où est allé votre mari ?

— Mon mari est allé-z-en guerre,
Ah ! je ne sais s'il reviendra.

— Marianson, dame jolie,
Prêtez-moi vos anneaux dorés.

— Il sont dans l'coffre, au pied du lit ;
Ah ! prends les clefs et va les qu'ri'.

— Bel orfèvrier, bel orfèvrier,
Faites-moi des anneaux dorés.

Qu'ils soyent faits aussi parfaits
Comm' les ceux' de Marianson.

MARIANSON.

"Ah, Marianson, my beauteous dame,
Where is your lord and master gone?"

"My lord rides to the battle-plain,
I know not if he'll come again."

"Ah, Marianson, my lady fair,
Lend me your rings of gold so rare."

"In the iron chest beside my bed,
You'll find the rings," she sweetly said.

"Now, Goldsmith, fashion me with care
Three golden rings of metal rare.

Three golden rings of fashion rare,
Like those that Marianson doth wear."

Quand il a eu ses trois anneaux,
Sur son cheval est embarqué.

Le premier qu'il a rencontré,
C'était l'mari d'Marianson.

— Ah ! bonjour donc, franc cavalier !
Quell' nouvell' m'as-tu apportée ?

Ah ! des nouvell's je n'en ai pas,
Que les ceux de Marianson.

— Marianson, dame jolie,
Ell' m'a été fidèle assez.

— Oui, je le crois, je le décrois :
Voilà les anneaux de ses doits.

— Tu as menti ! franc cavalier :
Ma femme m'est fidèle assez.

Sa femm' qu'était sur les remparts,
Et qui le voit venir là-bas :

When he receives his golden rings
Upon his steed he lightly springs.

The first he meets upon the road
Is Marianson's haughty lord.

" Fair greeting now, bold cavalier,
What tidings do you bring me here?"

" Of tidings new I bring you none,
Save of the Lady Marianson."

" Ah, Marianson, my lady fair !
She's faithful aye, I'll boldly swear."

" I say not 'yes,'—I say not ' no,'
But see—the rings from her hands of snow."

" You lie ! you lie ! bold cavalier :
My wife is faithful, far or near."

His wife stood on the ramparts high :
She saw her lord ride wildly by.

—Il est malade ou bien fâché,
C'est une chos' bien assurée.

Ah ! maman, montre-lui son fils :
Ça lui rejouira l'esprit.

— Ah ! tiens, mon fils, voilà ton fils.
Quel nom donn'ras-tu à ton fils ?

— A l'enfant je donn'rai un nom,
A la mère, un mauvais renom.

A pris l'enfant par le maillot,
Trois fois par terre il l'a jeté.

Marianson, par les cheveux,
A son cheval l'a-t-attachée.

Il a marché trois jours, trois nuits,
Sans regarder derrier' lui.

Au bout des trois jours et trois nuits,
A regardé par derrier' lui.

Her heart stood still with a sudden fear
When she marked his face as he drew anear.

" Now, mother, show our new-born child,
Its grace will calm his anger wild."

"My son, behold your son and heir :
What name wilt thou give the babe to bear?"

He cried, " I'll give the child a name
That will fill its mother's life with shame."

He has seized the infant in its mirth,
And thrice has dashed it to the earth.

And Marianson, that lady fair,
He has tied to his horse by her golden hair.

Three days, three nights, he rode like wind,
And never cast a look behind.

Till, at close of the third long night,
He turned and looked on that awful sight.

— Marianson, dame jolie,
Où sont les anneaux de tes doigts ?

— Ils sont dans l'coffre, au pied du lit,
Ah ! prends les clefs et va les qu'ri.

Il n'eut pas fait trois tours de clef,
Les trois anneaux d'or a trouvés.

— Marianson, dame jolie,
Quel bon chirurgien vous faut-il ?

— Le bon chirurgien qu'il me faut,
C'est un bon drap pour m'ensev'lir.

— Marianson, dame jolie,
Votre mort m'est-elle pardonnée ?

— Oui, ma mort vous est pardonnée,
Non pas la cell' du nouveau-né...

"Ah, Marianson, my lady fair,
Where are your golden rings so rare?"

"In the iron chest, beside my bed,
You'll find the rings," she sadly said.

He has ta'en the keys with an evil grace,
And has found the rings in their hiding place.

"Ah, Marianson, my lady fair,
You shall have the best chirurgeon's care."

"The best chirurgeon I would crave
Is a fine white sheet for my quiet grave."

"Ah, Marianson, my beauteous dame,
Will God e'er pardon all my shame?"

"My death is pardoned now," she smiled,
"But never that of our helpless child."

JAMAIS JE NOURRIRAI DE GEAI.

J'E bien nourri le geai sept ans
    Dedans ma cage ronde ;
Au bout de la septième année,
Mon geai a pris son vol.
      O, gai !
Jamais je nourrirai de geai,
De geai jamais je nourrirai.

Au bout de la septième année
Mon geai a pris son vol.
— Reviens mon geai, mon joli geai,
Dedans ma cage ronde.

Reviens mon geai, mon joli geai,
Dedans ma cage ronde ;
Mon petit geai me fit réponse :
— Je veux faire le drôle.

JAMAIS JE NOURRIRAI DE GEAI.

I kept my jay for seven years
   In my round cage so bright,
And at the end of seven years,
My sweet jay took his flight,
      O, gai !
I'll never keep a jay again,
Ah ! never more I'll keep a jay.

And at the end of seven years
My jay his flight has ta'en :
" Come back my jay, my pretty jay,
Come to your cage again.

Come back my jay, my pretty jay,
Come back once more to me,"
To which my saucy jay replied,
" I'll play tho madcap free."

63

Mon petit geai me fit réponse :
— Je veux faire le drôle.
Je m'en irai dedans Paris
Pour fonder une école.

Je m'en irai dedans Paris
Pour fonder une école .
Toutes les dames de Paris
Viendront à mon école.

Toutes les dames de Paris
Viendront à mon école.
Je choisirai la plus jolie
Je renverrai les autr's.

O, gai !
Jamais je nourrirai de geai,
De geai jamais je nourrirai.

" I'll play the madcap free for once,
For once I'll play the fool—
To Paris fair I'll straight repair
And there will found a school.

" To Paris fair I'll straight repair
And there a school will found,
To which all ladies fair will come
From all the city round.

" Oh ! all the ladies fair will come
Unto my school so gay :
I'll choose the fairest of them all,
And send the rest away."
   O gai !
  I'll never keep a jay again,
 Ah ! never more I'll keep a jay.

J'AI PERDU MON AMANT'.

LUI.

J'ai perdu mon amant'
    Et je m'en souci' guère ;
Le regret que j'en ai
Sera bientôt passé.
Je porterai le deuil
D'un habit de satin ;
Je verserai des larmes
    De vin.

ELLE.

Amant, que j't'ai donc fait
Que puiss' tant te déplaire ?
Est-c' que j't'ai pas aimé
Comm' tu l'as mérité ?
Je t'ai aimé, je t'aime,
Je t'aimerai toujours.
Pour toi mon cœur soupire
    Toujours.

66

J'AI PERDU MON AMANT'.

HE.

I'VE lost my Love, in sooth,
  For that my care is light ;
What small despite I feel
Will soon have vanished quite.
For mourning I will wear
A suit of satin fine,
My only tears shall be
    Of wine.

SHE.

What have I done, my Love,
That thus displeases thee?
Have I not loved thee, Dear,
As thou had'st right to be?
I've loved thee ; love thee now ;
I'll love thee, Dear, for aye.
For thee my heart shall beat
    Alway.

67

ELLE.

La maison de chez nous
C'est un lieu solitaire ;
On n'y voit pas souvent
Divertir nos amants.
Pour des amants qu'on aime,
Qu'on aim' si tendrement,
On aimerait les voire
    Souvent.

LUI.

Si j'étais hirondelle,
Vers toi, bell' demoiselle,
Par derrièr' ces rochers
J'irais prendr' ma volée.
Et dans ton sein, ma belle,
J'irais me reposer,
Pour raconter la peine
    Que j'ai.

SHE.

At home, the house is now
A solitary place,
Where one but seldom sees
The light of lover's face.
And those we love so well,
With all love's tender pain,
We love to dream we'll see
    Again.

HE.

Were I a swallow swift,
Towards thee, my heart's delight,
O'er all these rocky wilds
I'd quickly wing my flight.
There safe from all the storm,
Soft nestling in thy breast,
I'd tell thee all my pain,
    At rest.

D'OU VIENS-TU, BERGERE ?

—D'où viens-tu, bergère,
    D'où viens-tu ?
—Je viens de l'étable,
    De m'y promener ;
    J'ai vu un miracle
    Ce soir arrivé.

—Qu'as-tu vu, bergère,
    Qu'as-tu vu ?
—J'ai vu dans la crèche
    Un petit enfant
    Sur la paille fraîche
    Mis bien tendrement.

—Rien de plus, bergère,
    Rien de plus ?
—Saint' Marie, sa mère,
    Qui lui fait boir' du lait,
    Saint Joseph, son père,
    Qui tremble du froid.

" Whence art thou, my maiden,
    Whence art thou ? "
" I come from the stable
  Where this very night,
  I, a shepherd maiden,
  Saw a wondrous sight."

" What saw'st thou, my maiden,
    What saw'st thou ? "
" There within the manger
  A little babe I saw,
  Lying softly sleeping
  On the golden straw."

" Nothing more, my maiden,
    Nothing more? "
" I saw the Holy Mother
  The little baby hold,
  And the father, Joseph,
  A tremble with the cold."

—Rien de plus, bergère,
  Rien de plus ?
—Ya le bœuf et l'âne,
  Qui sont par devant,
  Avec leur haleine
  Réchauffent l'enfant.

—Rien de plus, bergère,
  Rien de plus ?
—Ya trois petits anges
  Descendus du ciel
  Chantant les louanges
  Du Père éternel.

" Nothing more, my maiden,
    Nothing more ? "
" I saw the ass and oxen
    Kneeling meek and mild,
    With their gentle breathing
    Warm the Holy Child."

" Nothing more, my maiden,
    Nothing more ? "
" There were three bright angels
    Come down from the sky
    Singing forth sweet praises
    To the Father high."

NOTES.

A LA CLAIRE FONTAINE.

This charming love story, with its attractive air, rightly heads our Canadian songs. It apparently enjoyed as great a popularity in France as here, for Dr. Larue cites no less than five variations of the words. Its origin is unknown, but it is sung in Normandy, Brittany and Franche-Comté.

" A few years ago," Dr. Larue says, "our *Claire Fontaine*, with its own Canadian air, was rendered in one of the principal theatres of Paris and obtained an immense success."

MALBROUCK.

In " Malbrouck" we have the song as it was sung in the time of *Le Grand Monarque*, with the English general and his army fighting brilliantly and swearing terribly in Flanders, while the people in Paris lilted his funeral elegy to the gay refrain of *Mironton, mirontaine*.

Dr. Larue traces it back to a similar burlesque elegy on the Duke of Guise, while Father Prout, in his Reliques, gives the popular tradition that it was composed by Mme.

de Sévigné as a cradle song for the Dauphin. Dumersan and Ségur, in a note quoted in John Oxenford's " French Songs," think that the words were probably brought back by the soldiers of Villars and Boufflers after Malplaquet. At all events verses against Marlborough were in existence in France in 1706.

The popularity of the old air, with the refrain of *Miron-ton, mirontaine,* is evinced by its survival among all English-speaking people wedded to the after-dinner sentiment of " He's a jolly good fellow."

It was a great favourite with Napoleon, and many a time it was hummed by him when mounting for battle. The Count de Las Cases, in the *Mémorial de Sainte Hélène* p. 821, tells the following :—The Emperor, a few weeks before his death, in speaking of this song to the Count, remarked, " ' What a thing ridicule is: it bedims everything, even victory.' And he laughed himself as he hummed over the first couplet." Of its popularity with military men, we Canadians have a later example in General Strange's reply to the 65th, a French-Canadian regiment, during the recent North-West rebellion. One morning, after weeks of tedious and toilsome marching, just as the men were about to fall in, the General overheard the remark—" Ah ! when will we go home," " Ah, mes garçons," laughed the General,

> " Malbrouck s'en va-t-en guerre,
> Mais quand reviendra-t-il ?"

and with their characteristic light-heartedness the men caught up the famous old air and the march was resumed without a murmur.

At least five different airs are sung in Canada, and in one the curious refrain " *Spiritum sanctum tuum*" is substituted for *Mironton, mirontaine* ; while the most popular version has the chorus,

> *Courez, courez, courez,*
> *Mes petit's filles, jeun's et gentilles,*
> *Courez, courez, courez,*
> *Venez ce soir vous amuser.*

LE POMMIER DOUX.

The air of *Le pommier doux* is familiar to French and English alike, and with its modern words and title of *Vive la Canadienne* has been very generally accepted as our national air. It is sung in Franche-Comté, but to an air different from ours, and lacking the verse *Les feuilles en sont vertes*, which is so decided an addition to our Canadian song.

EN ROULANT MA BOULE.

This is sung in the Departments of the West with a number of different refrains, some of which are quoted in Gagnon. As a popular song in Canada it ranks next to *La claire fontaine.*

GAI LE ROSIER

Is sung in Saintonge and Bas-Pitou.

BRIGADIER.

This, of course, is not a Canadian song at all, and has no claims to antiquity, but any collection would be sadly imperfect if our friend Pandore with his reassuring response were omitted.

It is extremely difficult to render the current of burlesque sentiment which runs through the original, so fine indeed, that it is almost invariably overlooked by those who know the song familiarly; the magnificent swing of the music is probably the cause of its being so frequently rendered *au serieux.*

DANS LES PRISONS DE NANTES.

M. Gagnon says that this charming ballad has disappeared entirely in France.

CECILIA

Is sung in Champagne, and Dr. Larue states that the air, as given in Champfleury, is exactly the same as that sung in Canada.

C'ETAIT UNE FREGATE.

This is a variation of *Isabeau s'y promène,* and was discovered by M. Gagnon : *Isabeau* is sung in Champagne.

ENTRE PARIS ET ST. DENIS.

The story in this song is the best evidence of its age. In the translation the word Nantes has been accented (Nan-tés) to give it an equivalent value in English.

MARIANSON.

Here we have the middle ages, with all their brutality and crime, unrelieved by any glamour of chivalry or ro-

F

mance. The ballad seems to have been preserved in its original entirety; at least the dreadful tale of treason and murder is told with dramatic completeness in the rude and irregular couplets, which are in themselves a proof of its age.

It will be noticed that there is no burden or refrain.

JAMAIS JE NOURRIRAI DE GEAI.

The origin of this song was apparently unknown to M. Gagnon, and perhaps, as Dr. Larue suggests in the case of *La claire fontaine*, it was not made at all,—it simply grew.

J'AI PERDU MON AMANT'.

Among the popular songs preserved here it is a surprise to come across so great a contrast to their general tone and feeling as this familiar lover's quarrel, which has come down to us as bright as the summer's day on which it happened so long ago. And yet a popular song it undoubtedly is and may be found in all collections with slight variations of the words, the best evidence, however, being that M. Gagnon discovered it in the County of Maskinongé.

D'OU VIENS-TU, BERGERE ?

A more simple and perfect example of the old *noël* than this, would be difficult to find. The melody has the same simplicity as the words and is well worth preservation as a Christmas hymn.

Michelet's remark, quoted by M. Gagnon, well illustrates the origin of the *noël*.—

" In those days, a marvellous dramatic talent, frequently stamped with a childish simplicity but full of boldness and kindliness, existed in the Church... At times she made herself little ; she, the great, the learned, the eternal, babbled with her children and translated the ineffable for them into a language they could understand."